™

STONE ARCH BOOKS
a capstone imprint

▼▼ STONE ARCH BOOKS™

Published in 2013
A Capstone Imprint
1710 Roe Crest Drive
North Mankato, MN 56003
www.capstonepub.com

Originally published by DC Comics in
the U.S. in single magazine form as
DC Super Friends #5.
Copyright © 2013 DC Comics. All Rights Reserved.

Cataloging-in-Publication Data is available at the
Library of Congress website:
ISBN: 978-1-4342-4700-1 (library binding)

Summary: The entire world has gone ape, and the
Super Friends better find out why! So it's off to
Gorilla City for a mystery so exciting, you'll go
bananas!

STONE ARCH BOOKS

Ashley C. Andersen Zantop *Publisher*
Michael Dahl *Editorial Director*
Donald Lemke & Julie Gassman *Editors*
Heather Kindseth *Creative Director*
Brann Garvey *Designer*
Kathy McColley *Production Specialist*

DC COMICS
Rachel Gluckstern *Original U.S. Editor*

Printed in China by Nordica.
1012/CA21201277
092012   006935NORDS13

DC Comics
1700 Broadway, New York, NY 10019
A Warner Bros. Entertainment Company

DC Super Friends

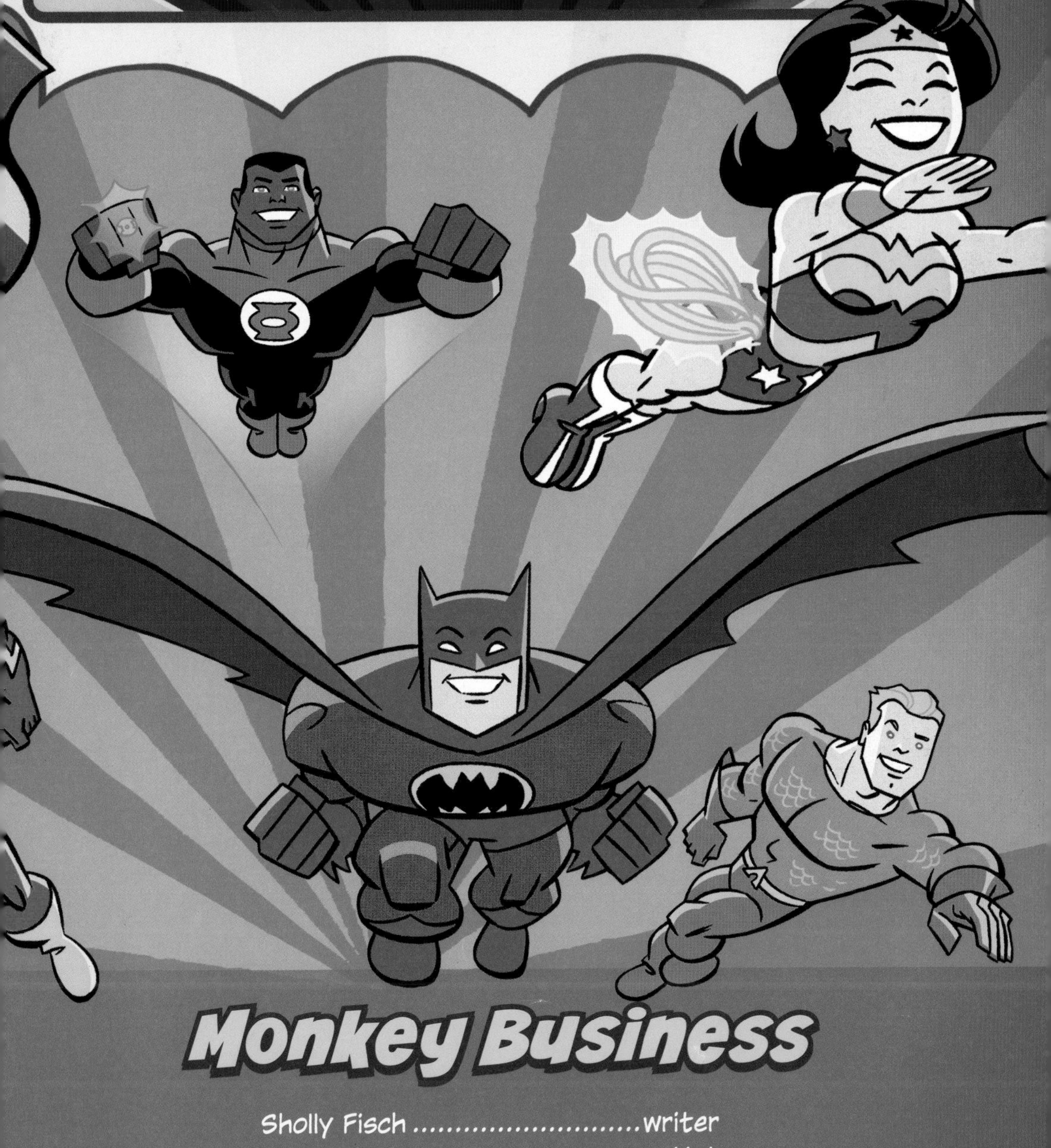

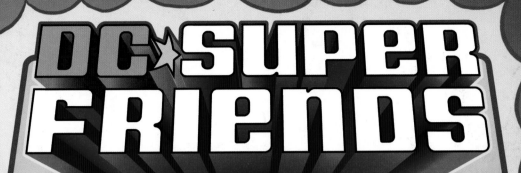

Monkey Business

Sholly Fisch .... writer
Stewart McKenny .... artist
Phil Moy...................................... inker
Heroic Age .... colorist
Travis Lanham .... letterer
J. Bone .... cover artist

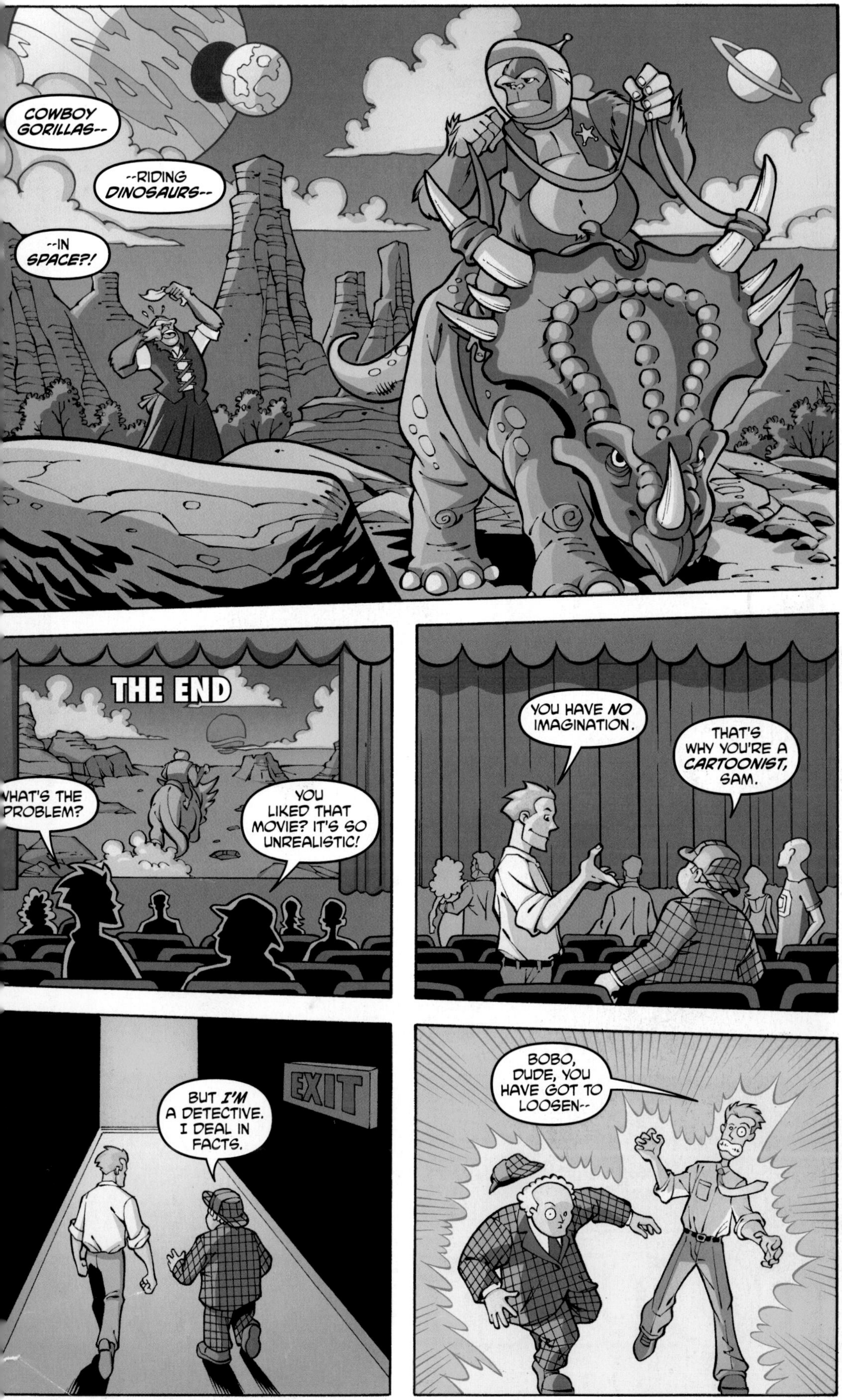
COWBOY GORILLAS--
--RIDING DINOSAURS--
--IN SPACE?!
THE END
WHAT'S THE PROBLEM?
YOU LIKED THAT MOVIE? IT'S SO UNREALISTIC!
YOU HAVE NO IMAGINATION.
THAT'S WHY YOU'RE A CARTOONIST, SAM.
EXIT
BUT I'M A DETECTIVE. I DEAL IN FACTS.
BOBO, DUDE, YOU HAVE GOT TO LOOSEN--

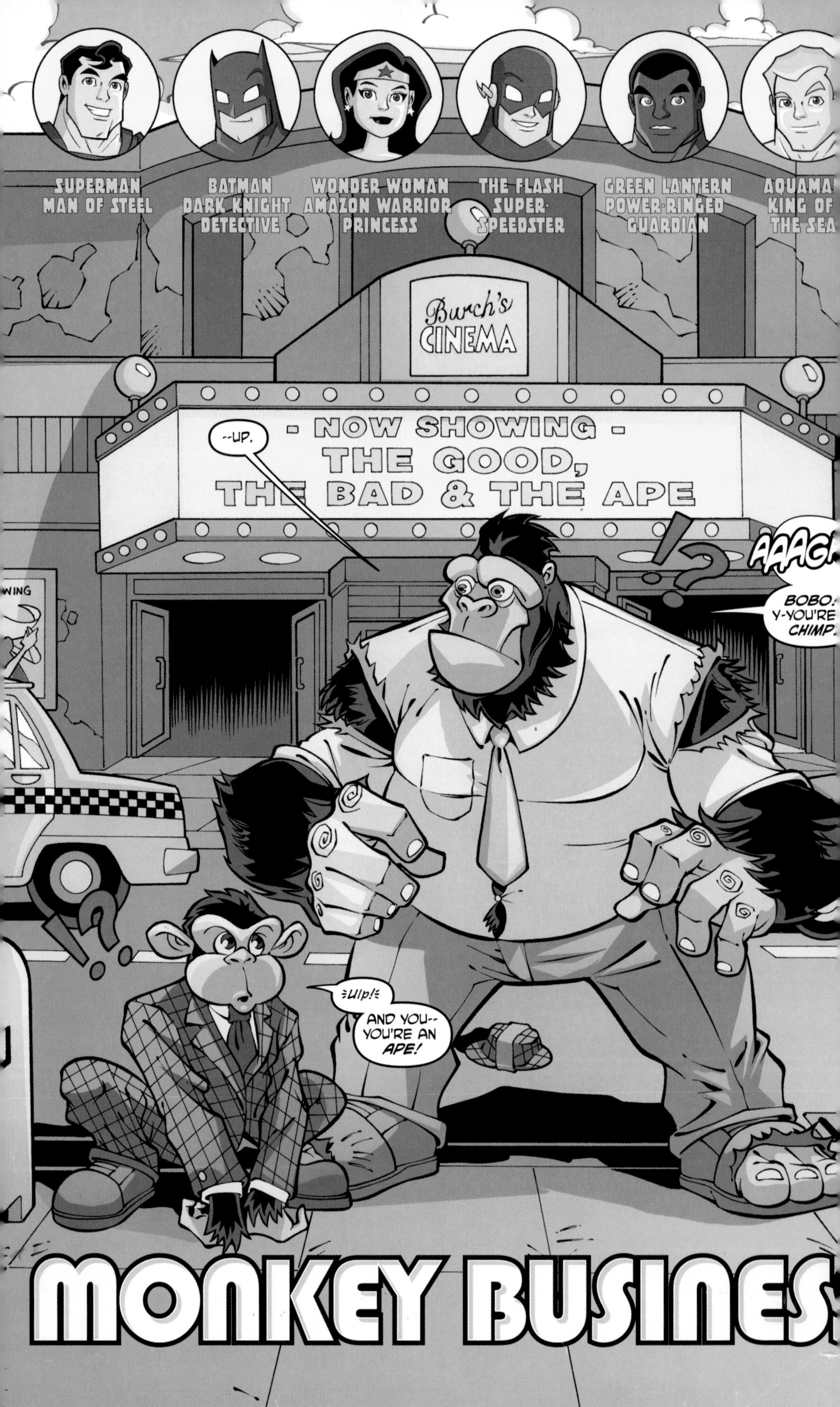

SUPERMAN MAN OF STEEL
BATMAN DARK KNIGHT DETECTIVE
WONDER WOMAN AMAZON WARRIOR PRINCESS
THE FLASH SUPER-SPEEDSTER
GREEN LANTERN POWER-RINGED GUARDIAN
AQUAMA KING OF THE SEA
Burch's CINEMA
- NOW SHOWING - THE GOOD, THE BAD & THE APE
--UP.
AAAG
BOBO! Y-YOU'RE CHIMP!
ULP!
AND YOU-- YOU'RE AN APE!
MONKEY BUSINES

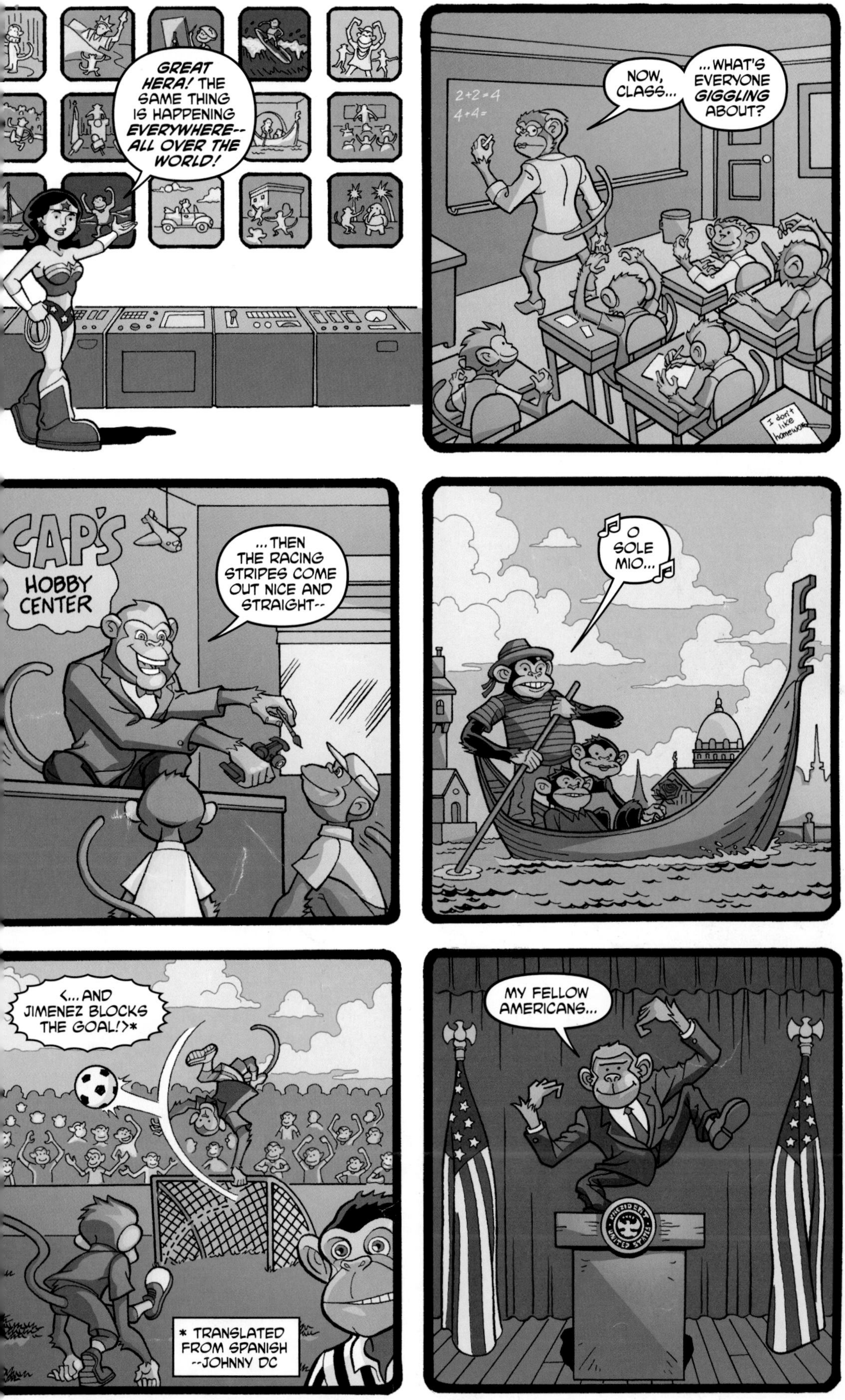
GREAT HERA! THE SAME THING IS HAPPENING EVERYWHERE-- ALL OVER THE WORLD!
2+2=4
4+4=
NOW, CLASS...
...WHAT'S EVERYONE GIGGLING ABOUT?
I don't like homework
CAP'S HOBBY CENTER
...THEN THE RACING STRIPES COME OUT NICE AND STRAIGHT--
O SOLE MIO...
<...AND JIMENEZ BLOCKS THE GOAL!>*
* TRANSLATED FROM SPANISH --JOHNNY DC
MY FELLOW AMERICANS...

THE SUPER FRIENDS' SATELLITE HEADQUARTERS--

YOU MEAN *EVERYONE* ON *EARTH* HAS TURNED INTO SOME KIND OF *APE*?

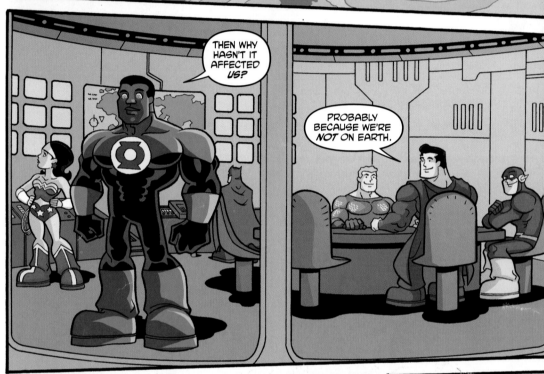

THEN WHY HASN'T IT AFFECTED *US*?

PROBABLY BECAUSE WE'RE *NOT* ON EARTH.

SO WHEN *WE* RETURN TO EARTH, WE'LL PROBABLY TURN INTO *APES*?

COOL!

"COOL"?

HEY, I'VE ALREADY BEEN TURNED INTO A *MIRROR,* A *BOOMERANG,* AND A *PUPPET!*

AFTER ALL THAT, AN APE WOULD BE A STEP UP!

HMM... IF WE KNEW WHAT *CAUSED* THIS, WE MIGHT BE ABLE TO *STOP* IT.

THAT'S WHY I'M MAKING A CHART OF *WHEN* DIFFERENT PEOPLE TURNED INTO APES.

IT LOOKS LIKE IT *STARTED* SOMEWHERE IN *AFRICA.*

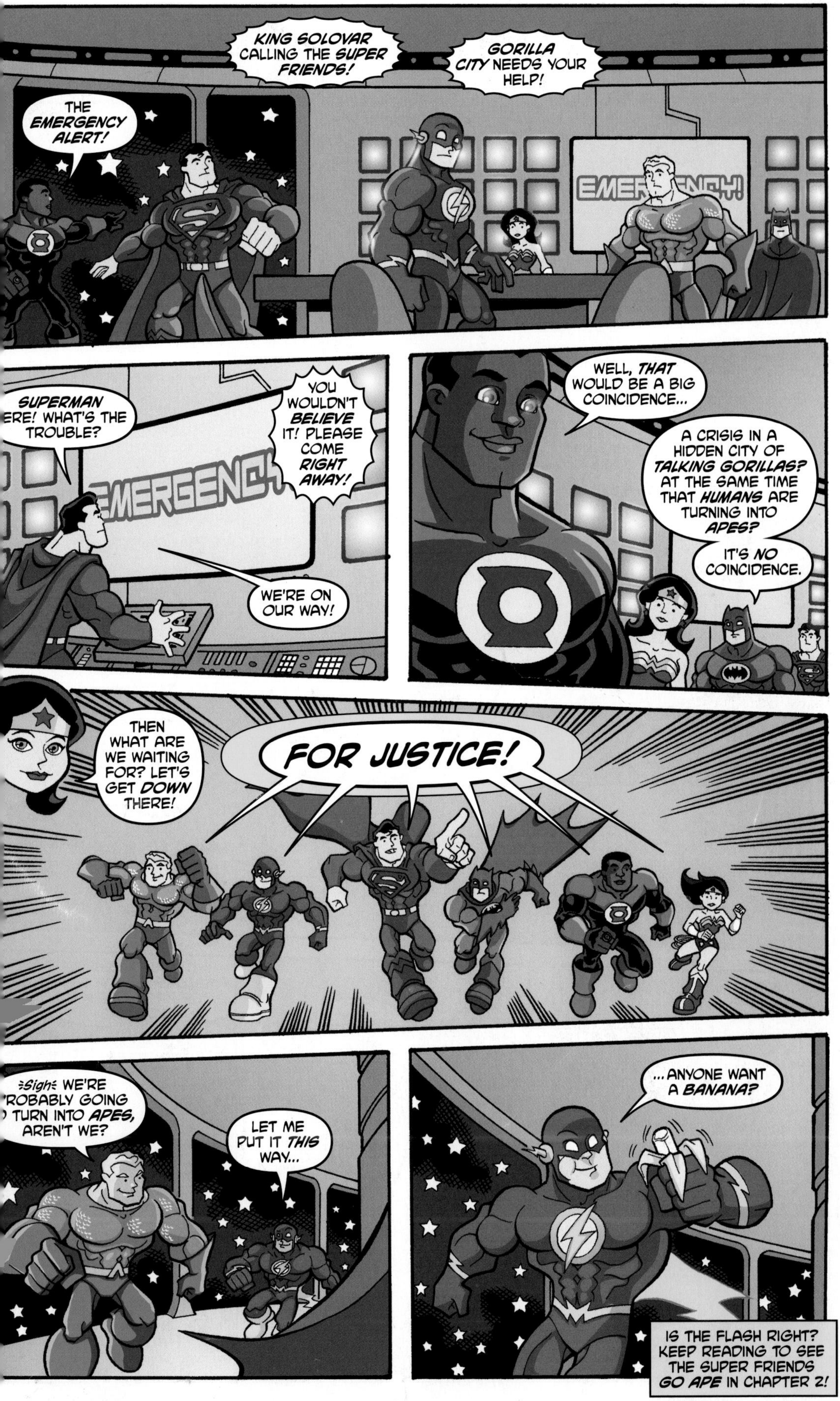
THE EMERGENCY ALERT!
KING SOLOVAR CALLING THE SUPER FRIENDS!
GORILLA CITY NEEDS YOUR HELP!
SUPERMAN ERE! WHAT'S THE TROUBLE?
YOU WOULDN'T BELIEVE IT! PLEASE COME RIGHT AWAY!
WE'RE ON OUR WAY!
WELL, THAT WOULD BE A BIG COINCIDENCE...
A CRISIS IN A HIDDEN CITY OF TALKING GORILLAS? AT THE SAME TIME THAT HUMANS ARE TURNING INTO APES?
IT'S NO COINCIDENCE.
THEN WHAT ARE WE WAITING FOR? LET'S GET DOWN THERE!
FOR JUSTICE!
Sigh WE'RE ROBABLY GOING TURN INTO APES, AREN'T WE?
LET ME PUT IT THIS WAY...
...ANYONE WANT A BANANA?
IS THE FLASH RIGHT? KEEP READING TO SEE THE SUPER FRIENDS GO APE IN CHAPTER 2!

MONKEY BUSINESS CHAPTER

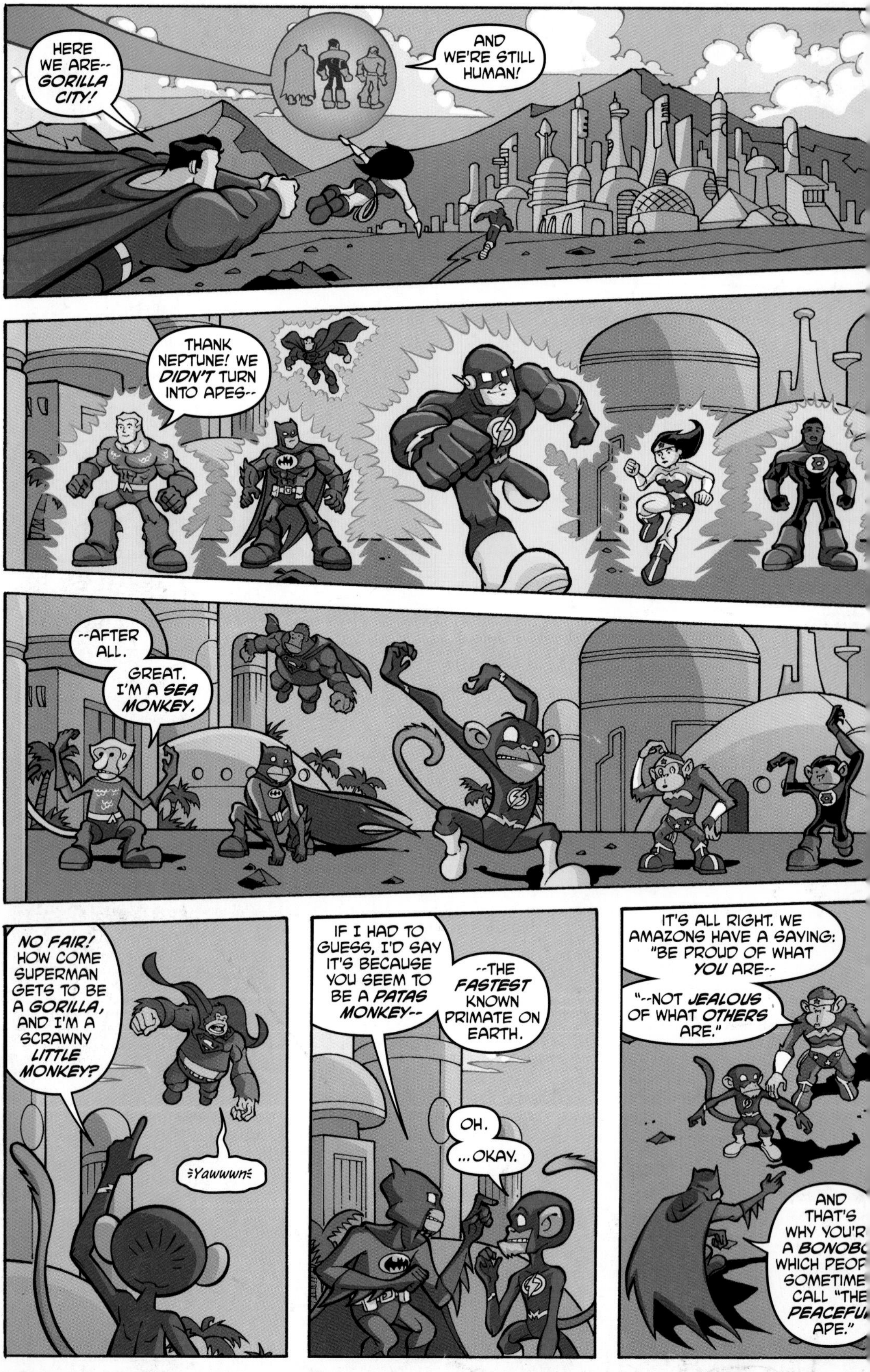

HERE WE ARE-- GORILLA CITY!
AND WE'RE STILL HUMAN!
THANK NEPTUNE! WE DIDN'T TURN INTO APES--
--AFTER ALL.
GREAT. I'M A SEA MONKEY.
NO FAIR! HOW COME SUPERMAN GETS TO BE A GORILLA, AND I'M A SCRAWNY LITTLE MONKEY?
Yawwwn
IF I HAD TO GUESS, I'D SAY IT'S BECAUSE YOU SEEM TO BE A PATAS MONKEY--
--THE FASTEST KNOWN PRIMATE ON EARTH.
OH.
...OKAY.
IT'S ALL RIGHT. WE AMAZONS HAVE A SAYING: "BE PROUD OF WHAT YOU ARE--
"--NOT JEALOUS OF WHAT OTHERS ARE."
AND THAT'S WHY YOU'R A BONOB WHICH PEOP SOMETIME CALL "THE PEACEFU APE."

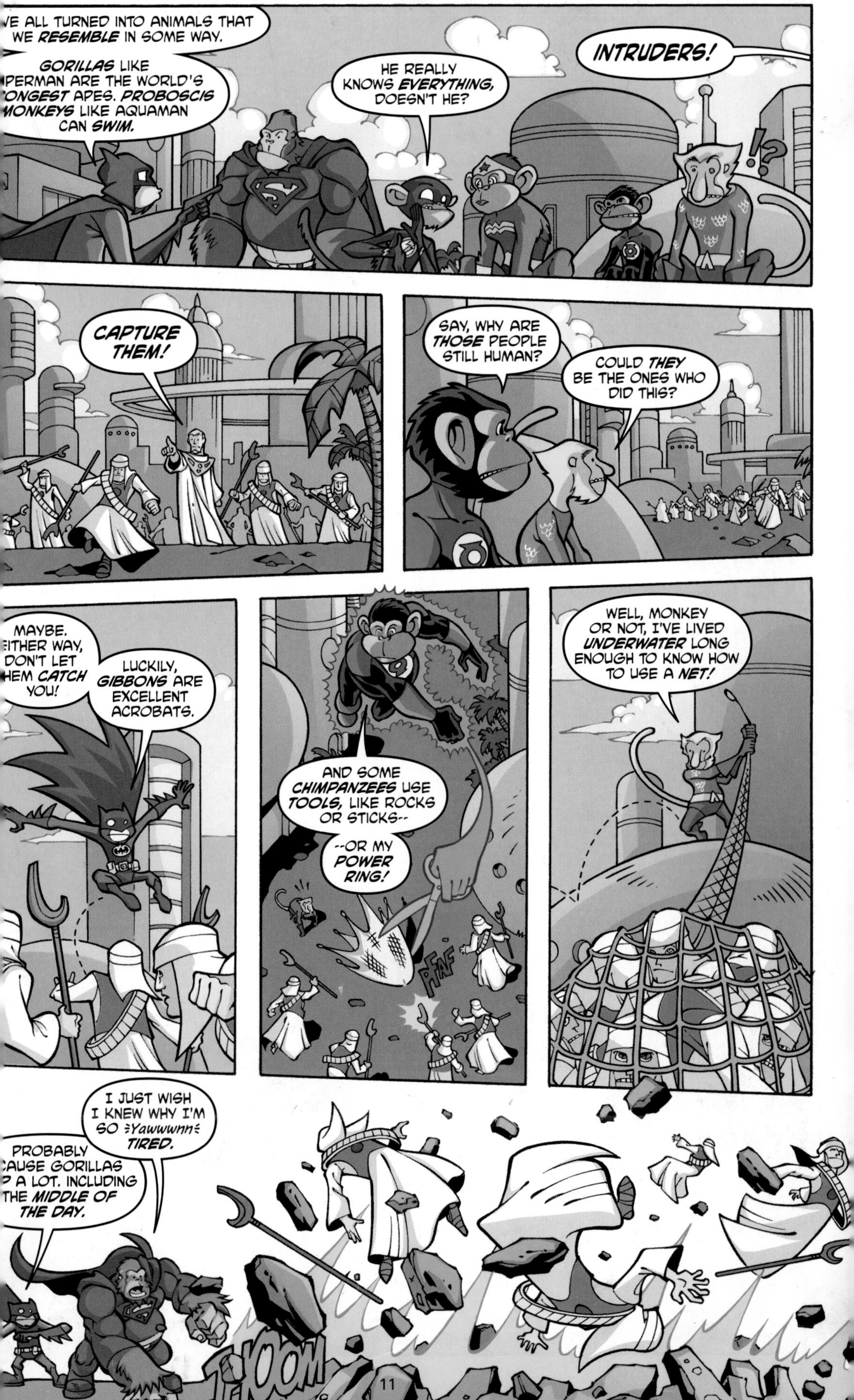

VE ALL TURNED INTO ANIMALS THAT WE RESEMBLE IN SOME WAY.
GORILLAS LIKE PERMAN ARE THE WORLD'S ONGEST APES. PROBOSCIS MONKEYS LIKE AQUAMAN CAN SWIM.
HE REALLY KNOWS EVERYTHING, DOESN'T HE?
INTRUDERS!
!?
CAPTURE THEM!
SAY, WHY ARE THOSE PEOPLE STILL HUMAN?
COULD THEY BE THE ONES WHO DID THIS?
MAYBE. EITHER WAY, DON'T LET HEM CATCH YOU!
LUCKILY, GIBBONS ARE EXCELLENT ACROBATS.
AND SOME CHIMPANZEES USE TOOLS, LIKE ROCKS OR STICKS--
--OR MY POWER RING!
PFAF
WELL, MONKEY OR NOT, I'VE LIVED UNDERWATER LONG ENOUGH TO KNOW HOW TO USE A NET!
I JUST WISH I KNEW WHY I'M SO Yawwwnn TIRED.
PROBABLY CAUSE GORILLAS P A LOT. INCLUDING THE MIDDLE OF THE DAY.
THOOM

THAT'S THE *LAST* OF THEM!

NOW, PERHAPS WE CAN FIND OUT WHAT'S GOING ON.

BAH! YOU INVADERS MAY BE WINNING *NOW*, BUT YOU WILL *NEVER* CONQUER GORILLA CITY!

WE WILL *PROTECT* OUR CITY, AS SURE AS MY NAME IS *SOLOVAR!*

"SOLOVAR"? *YOU'RE* SOLOVAR?

SHOULDN'T YOU BE *HAIRIER?* AND, Y'KNOW, A *GORILLA?*

WE *WERE*, UNTIL THIS *MORN*--

HOLD ON! YOU'RE *REALLY* THE SUPER FRIENDS?

HOW DID YOU TURN INTO *APES?*

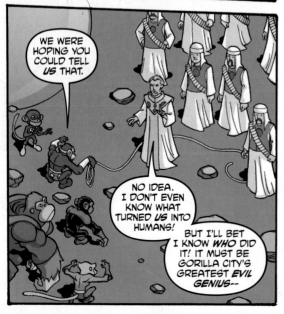

WE WERE HOPING YOU COULD TELL *US* THAT.

NO IDEA. I DON'T EVEN KNOW WHAT TURNED *US* INTO HUMANS!

BUT I'LL BET I KNOW *WHO* DID IT! IT MUST BE GORILLA CITY'S GREATEST *EVIL GENIUS*--

--GORILLA GRODD!

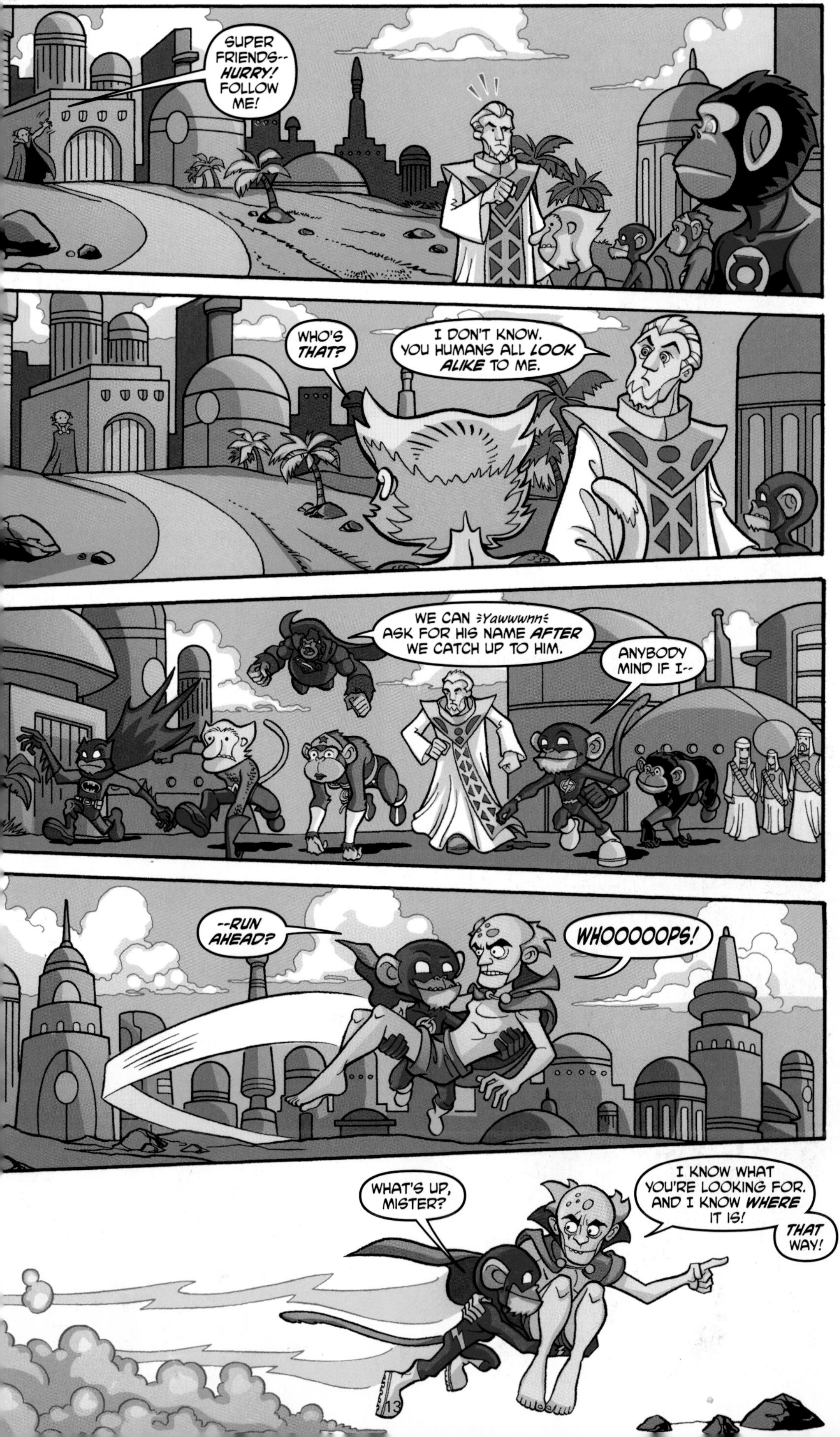

SUPER FRIENDS-- HURRY! FOLLOW ME!
WHO'S THAT?
I DON'T KNOW. YOU HUMANS ALL LOOK ALIKE TO ME.
WE CAN ≈Yawwwnn≈ ASK FOR HIS NAME AFTER WE CATCH UP TO HIM.
ANYBODY MIND IF I--
--RUN AHEAD?
WHOOOOOPS!
WHAT'S UP, MISTER?
I KNOW WHAT YOU'RE LOOKING FOR. AND I KNOW WHERE IT IS!
THAT WAY!

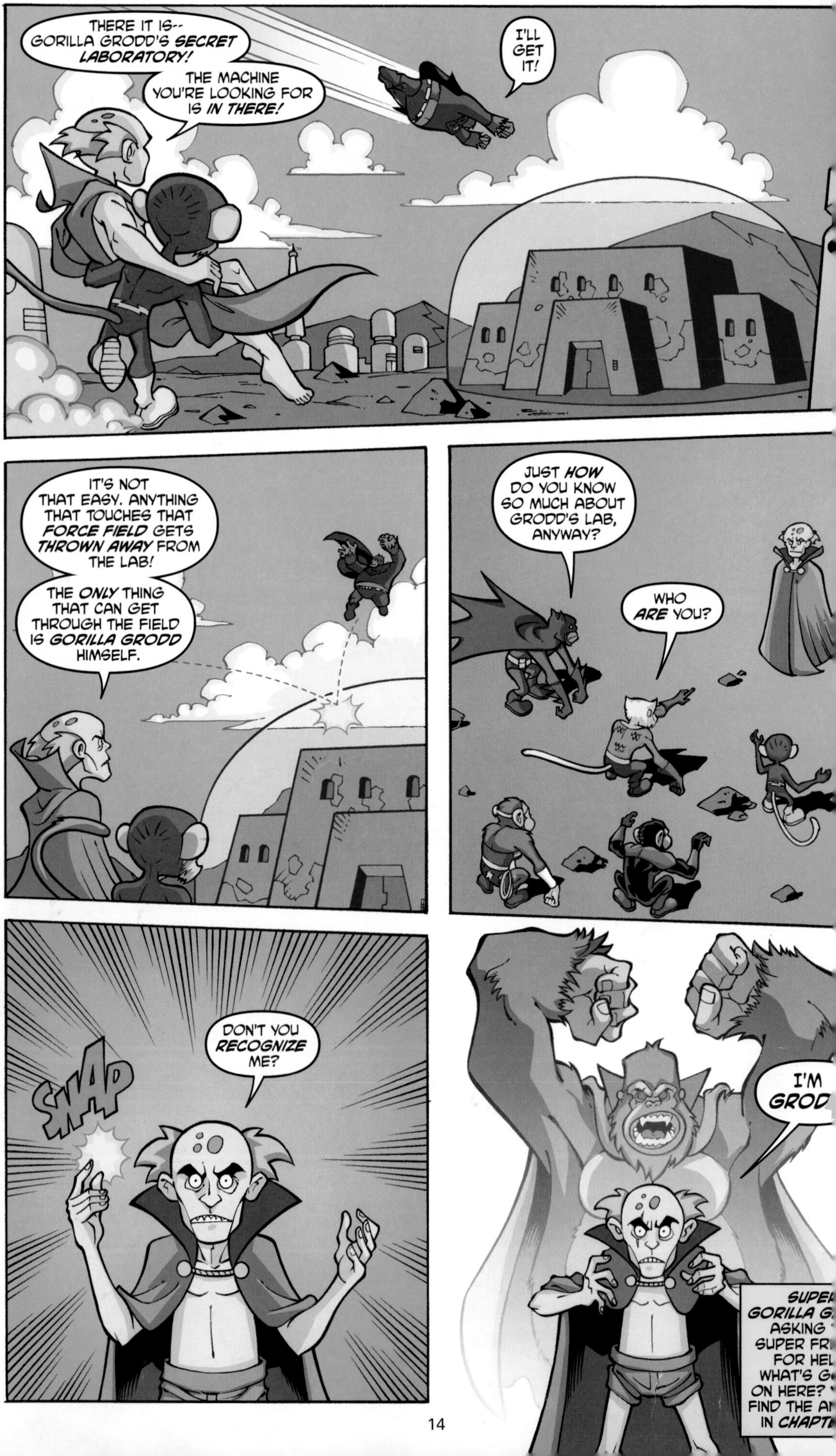

THERE IT IS-- GORILLA GRODD'S SECRET LABORATORY!
THE MACHINE YOU'RE LOOKING FOR IS IN THERE!
I'LL GET IT!
IT'S NOT THAT EASY. ANYTHING THAT TOUCHES THAT FORCE FIELD GETS THROWN AWAY FROM THE LAB!
THE ONLY THING THAT CAN GET THROUGH THE FIELD IS GORILLA GRODD HIMSELF.
JUST HOW DO YOU KNOW SO MUCH ABOUT GRODD'S LAB, ANYWAY?
WHO ARE YOU?
SNAP
DON'T YOU RECOGNIZE ME?
I'M GROD
SUPE GORILLA G ASKING SUPER FR FOR HEL WHAT'S G ON HERE? FIND THE A IN CHAPT

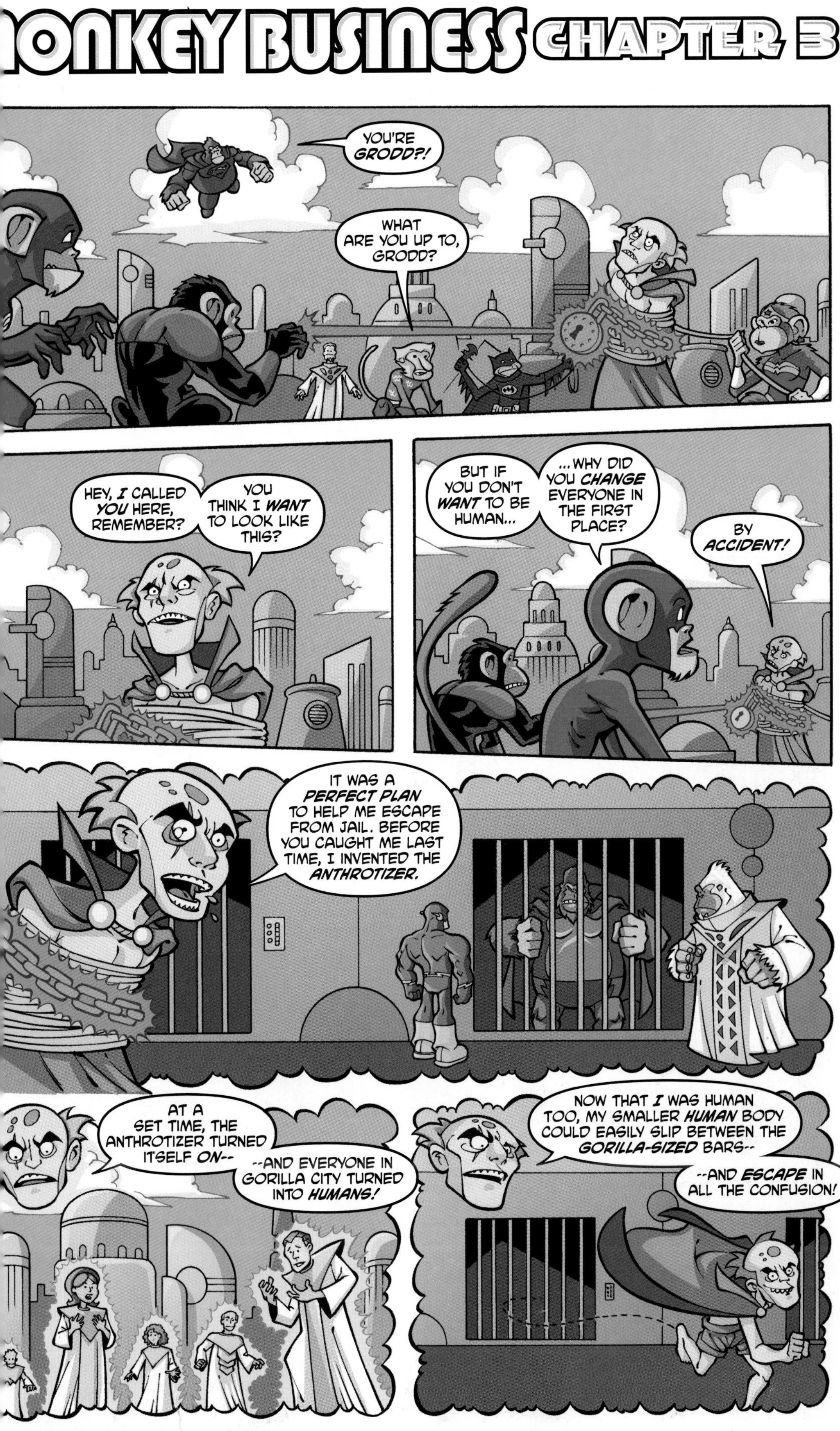
MONKEY BUSINESS CHAPTER 3
YOU'RE GRODD?!
WHAT ARE YOU UP TO, GRODD?
HEY, I CALLED YOU HERE, REMEMBER?
YOU THINK I WANT TO LOOK LIKE THIS?
BUT IF YOU DON'T WANT TO BE HUMAN...
...WHY DID YOU CHANGE EVERYONE IN THE FIRST PLACE?
BY ACCIDENT!
IT WAS A PERFECT PLAN TO HELP ME ESCAPE FROM JAIL. BEFORE YOU CAUGHT ME LAST TIME, I INVENTED THE ANTHROTIZER.
AT A SET TIME, THE ANTHROTIZER TURNED ITSELF ON--
--AND EVERYONE IN GORILLA CITY TURNED INTO HUMANS!
NOW THAT I WAS HUMAN TOO, MY SMALLER HUMAN BODY COULD EASILY SLIP BETWEEN THE GORILLA-SIZED BARS--
--AND ESCAPE IN ALL THE CONFUSION!

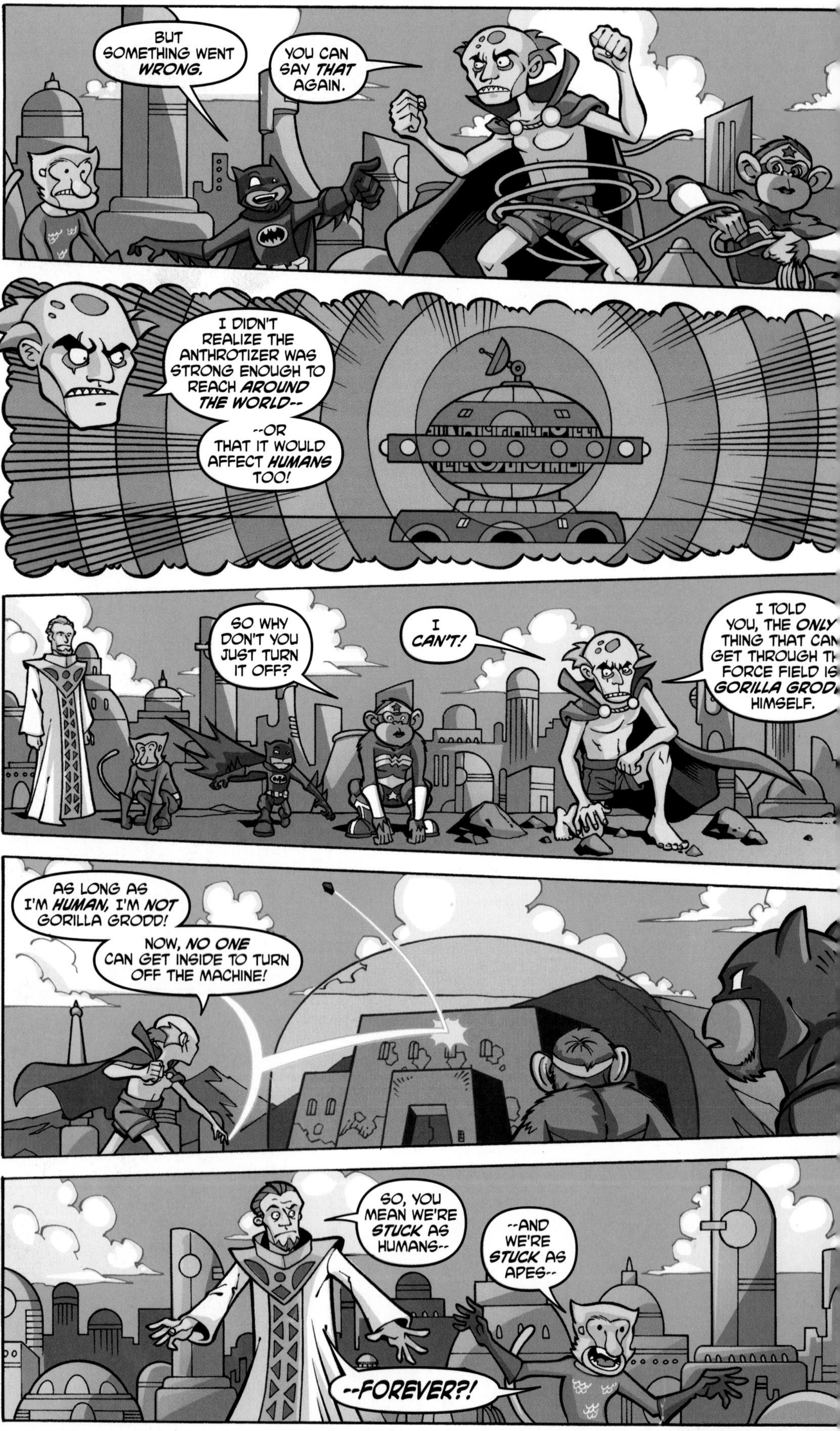
BUT SOMETHING WENT *WRONG.*
YOU CAN SAY *THAT* AGAIN.
I DIDN'T REALIZE THE ANTHROTIZER WAS STRONG ENOUGH TO REACH *AROUND THE WORLD--*
--OR THAT IT WOULD AFFECT *HUMANS* TOO!
SO WHY DON'T YOU JUST TURN IT OFF?
I *CAN'T!*
I TOLD YOU, THE *ONLY* THING THAT CAN GET THROUGH THE FORCE FIELD IS *GORILLA GRODD* HIMSELF.
AS LONG AS I'M *HUMAN,* I'M *NOT* GORILLA GRODD!
NOW, *NO ONE* CAN GET INSIDE TO TURN OFF THE MACHINE!
SO, YOU MEAN WE'RE *STUCK* AS HUMANS--
--AND WE'RE *STUCK* AS APES--
--FOREVER?!

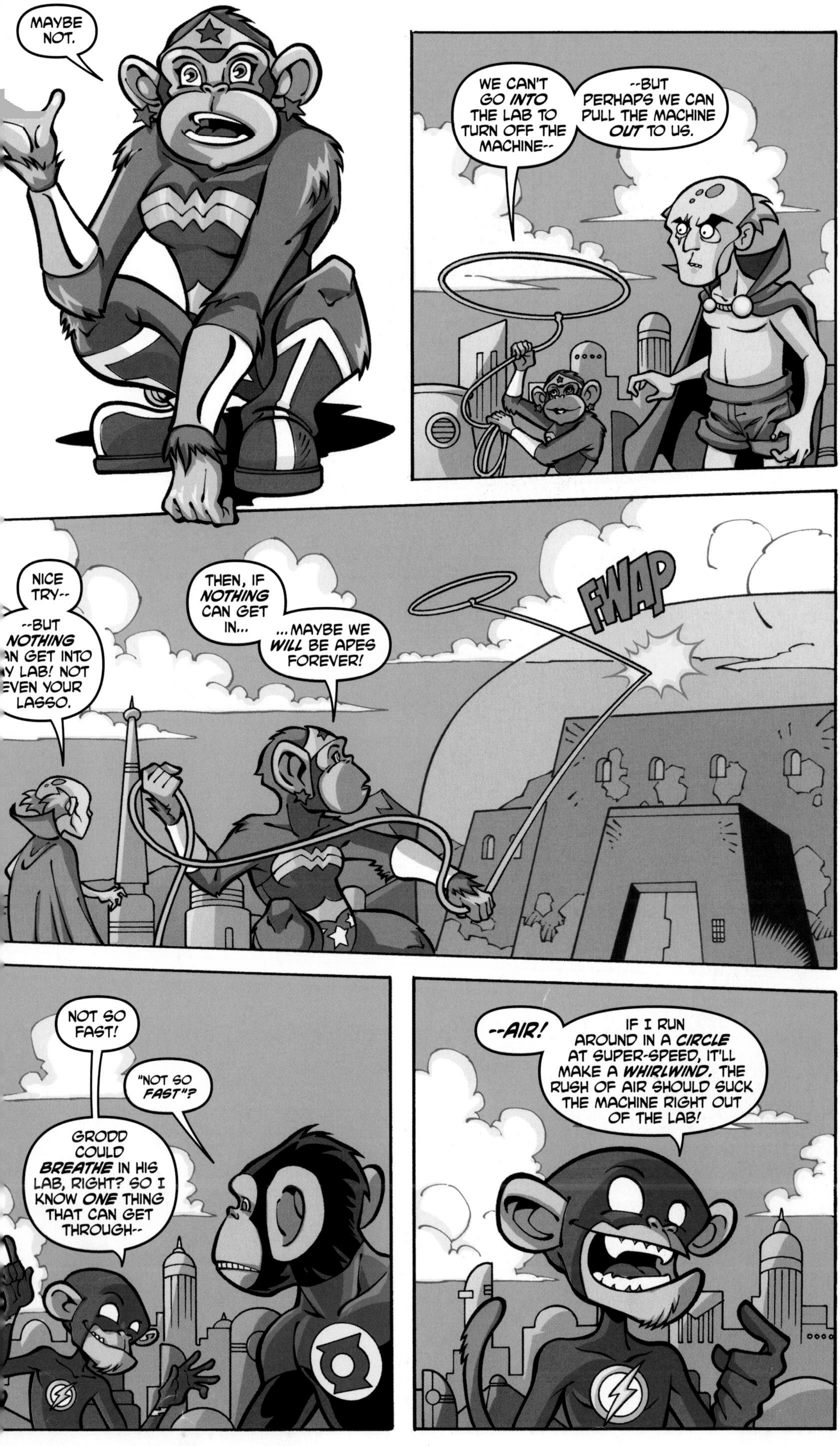
MAYBE NOT.
WE CAN'T GO INTO THE LAB TO TURN OFF THE MACHINE--
--BUT PERHAPS WE CAN PULL THE MACHINE OUT TO US.
NICE TRY--
--BUT NOTHING AN GET INTO Y LAB! NOT EVEN YOUR LASSO.
THEN, IF NOTHING CAN GET IN...
...MAYBE WE WILL BE APES FOREVER!
FWAP
NOT SO FAST!
"NOT SO FAST"?
GRODD COULD BREATHE IN HIS LAB, RIGHT? SO I KNOW ONE THING THAT CAN GET THROUGH--
--AIR!
IF I RUN AROUND IN A CIRCLE AT SUPER-SPEED, IT'LL MAKE A WHIRLWIND. THE RUSH OF AIR SHOULD SUCK THE MACHINE RIGHT OUT OF THE LAB!

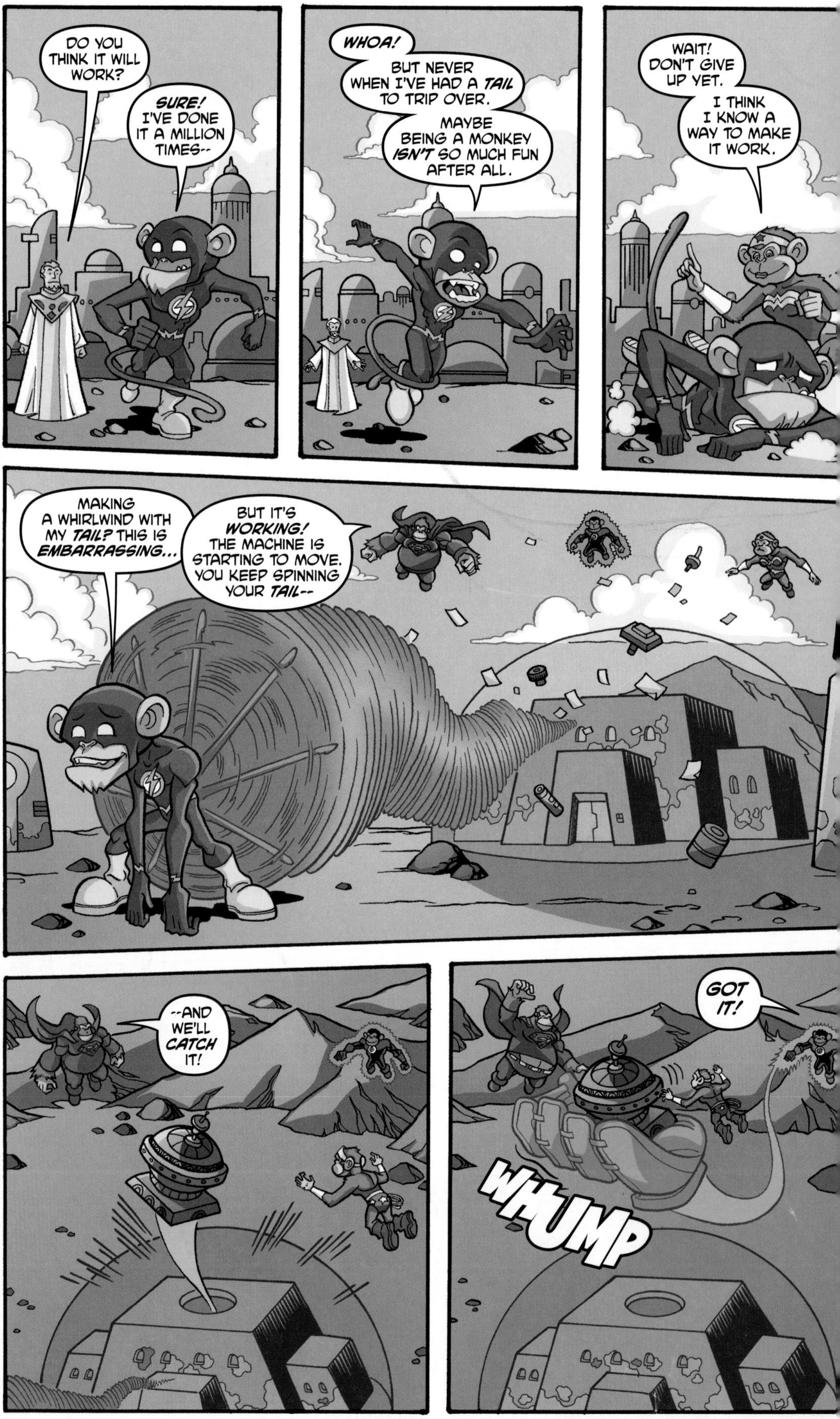
DO YOU THINK IT WILL WORK?
SURE! I'VE DONE IT A MILLION TIMES--
WHOA!
BUT NEVER WHEN I'VE HAD A TAIL TO TRIP OVER.
MAYBE BEING A MONKEY ISN'T SO MUCH FUN AFTER ALL.
WAIT! DON'T GIVE UP YET.
I THINK I KNOW A WAY TO MAKE IT WORK.
MAKING A WHIRLWIND WITH MY TAIL? THIS IS EMBARRASSING...
BUT IT'S WORKING! THE MACHINE IS STARTING TO MOVE. YOU KEEP SPINNING YOUR TAIL--
--AND WE'LL CATCH IT!
GOT IT!
WHUMP

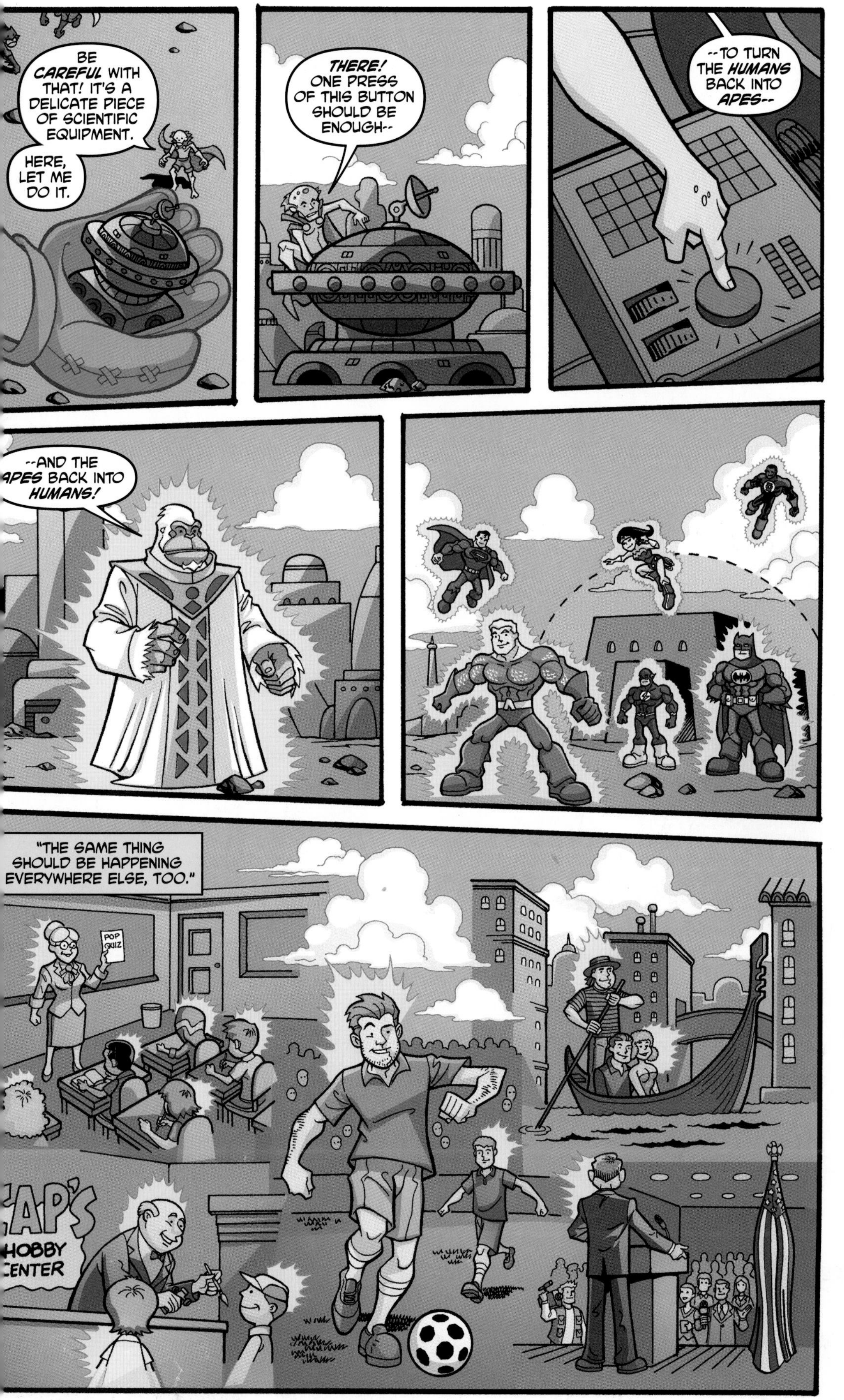
BE CAREFUL WITH THAT! IT'S A DELICATE PIECE OF SCIENTIFIC EQUIPMENT.
HERE, LET ME DO IT.
THERE! ONE PRESS OF THIS BUTTON SHOULD BE ENOUGH--
--TO TURN THE HUMANS BACK INTO APES--
--AND THE APES BACK INTO HUMANS!
"THE SAME THING SHOULD BE HAPPENING EVERYWHERE ELSE, TOO."
POP QUIZ
HOBBY CENTER

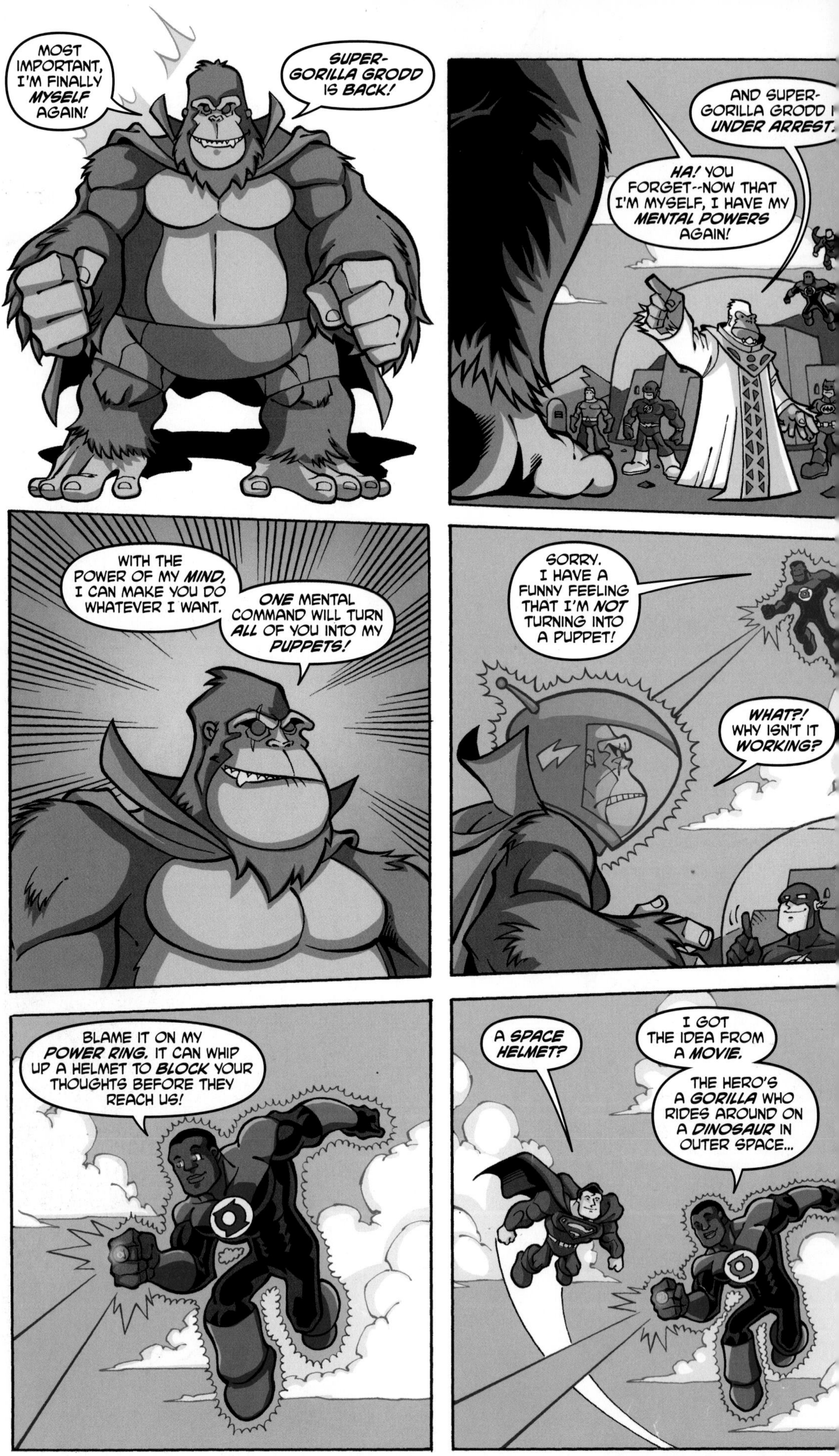

MOST IMPORTANT, I'M FINALLY MYSELF AGAIN!
SUPER-GORILLA GRODD IS BACK!
AND SUPER-GORILLA GRODD I UNDER ARREST.
HA! YOU FORGET--NOW THAT I'M MYSELF, I HAVE MY MENTAL POWERS AGAIN!
WITH THE POWER OF MY MIND, I CAN MAKE YOU DO WHATEVER I WANT.
ONE MENTAL COMMAND WILL TURN ALL OF YOU INTO MY PUPPETS!
SORRY. I HAVE A FUNNY FEELING THAT I'M NOT TURNING INTO A PUPPET!
WHAT?! WHY ISN'T IT WORKING?
BLAME IT ON MY POWER RING. IT CAN WHIP UP A HELMET TO BLOCK YOUR THOUGHTS BEFORE THEY REACH US!
A SPACE HELMET?
I GOT THE IDEA FROM A MOVIE.
THE HERO'S A GORILLA WHO RIDES AROUND ON A DINOSAUR IN OUTER SPACE...

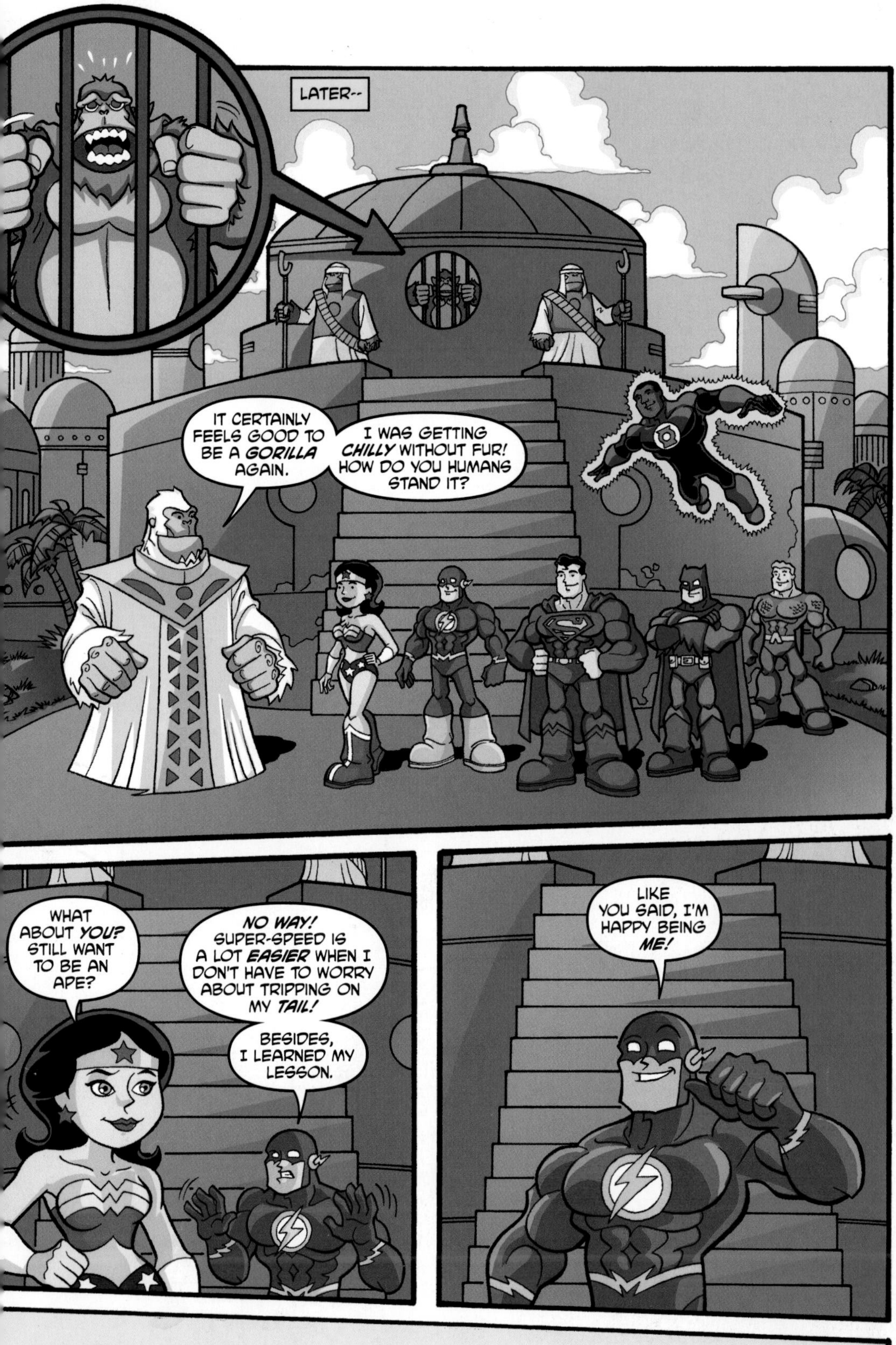
LATER--
IT CERTAINLY FEELS GOOD TO BE A GORILLA AGAIN.
I WAS GETTING CHILLY WITHOUT FUR! HOW DO YOU HUMANS STAND IT?
WHAT ABOUT YOU? STILL WANT TO BE AN APE?
NO WAY! SUPER-SPEED IS A LOT EASIER WHEN I DON'T HAVE TO WORRY ABOUT TRIPPING ON MY TAIL!
BESIDES, I LEARNED MY LESSON.
LIKE YOU SAID, I'M HAPPY BEING ME!

ATTENTION, ALL SUPER FRIENDS!

HERE'S THIS BOOK'S SECRET MESSAGE:

PEVOY CYSOXRP ZBBU BEI CBY BINOYP

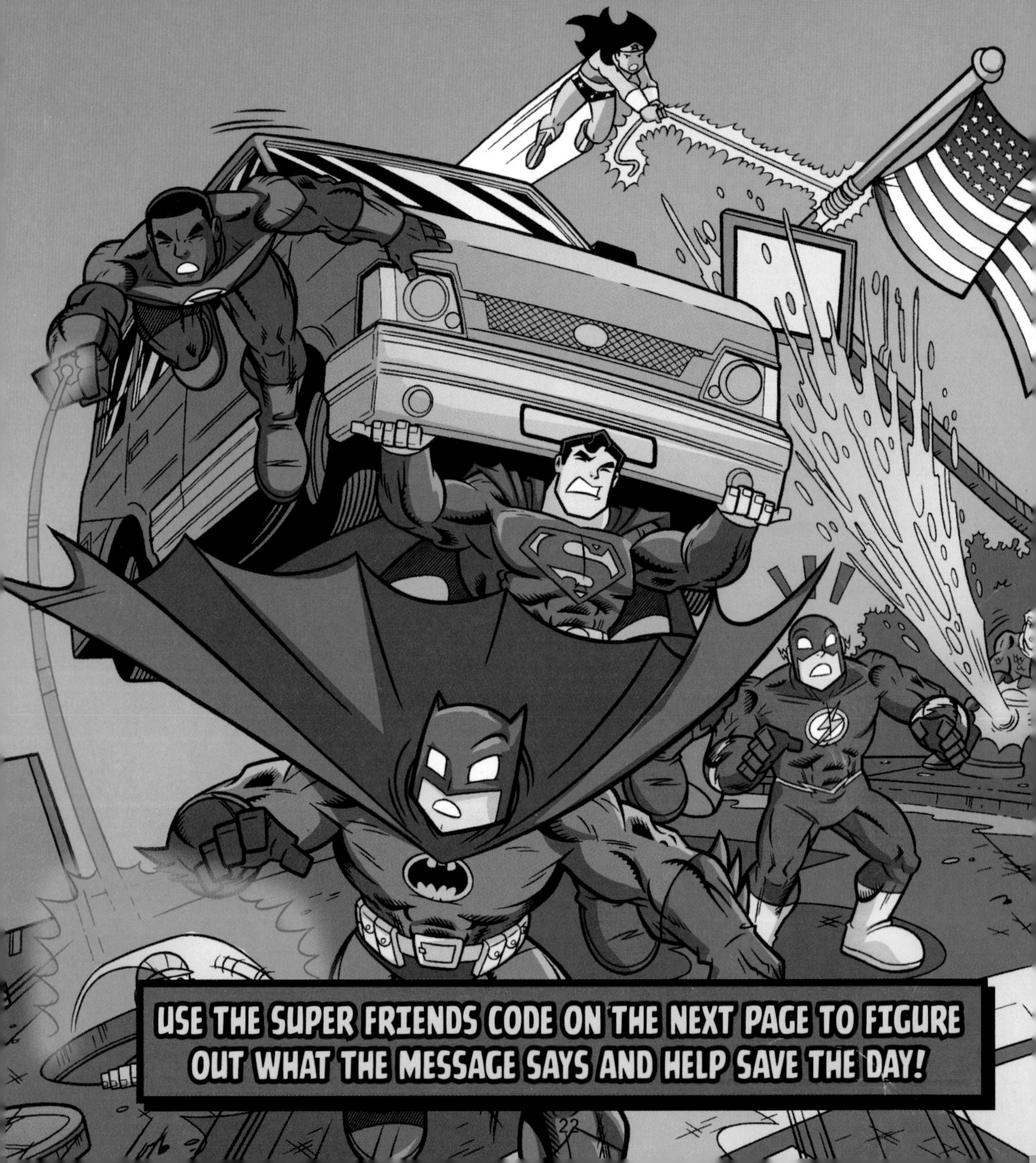

USE THE SUPER FRIENDS CODE ON THE NEXT PAGE TO FIGURE OUT WHAT THE MESSAGE SAYS AND HELP SAVE THE DAY!

HEY, SUPER FRIENDS! *YOU* CAN JOIN OUR TEAM--

--BY BEING A *SUPER FRIEND!*

BE KIND!

SHOW RESPECT!

HELP OUT!

DON'T FORGET TO USE THE CODE TO READ OUR *SECRET MESSAGES* IN EVERY ISSUE!

SUPER FRIENDS SECRET CODE
(KEEP THIS AWAY FROM SUPER-VILLAINS!)

J =
K =
L =
M =
N =
O =
P =
Q =
R =

S =
T =
U =
V =
W =
X =
Y =
Z =

KNOW YOUR SUPER FRIENDS!

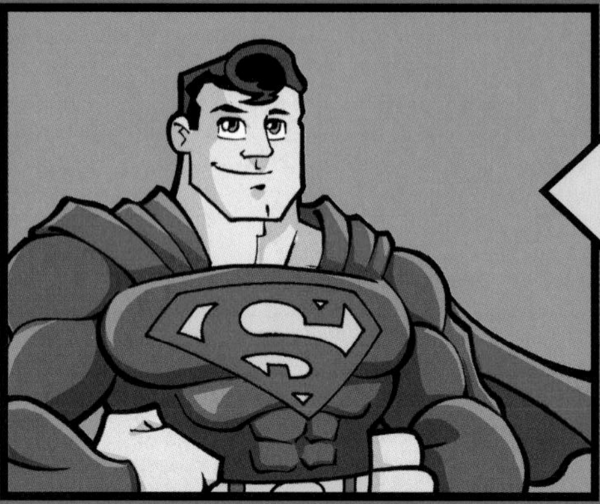

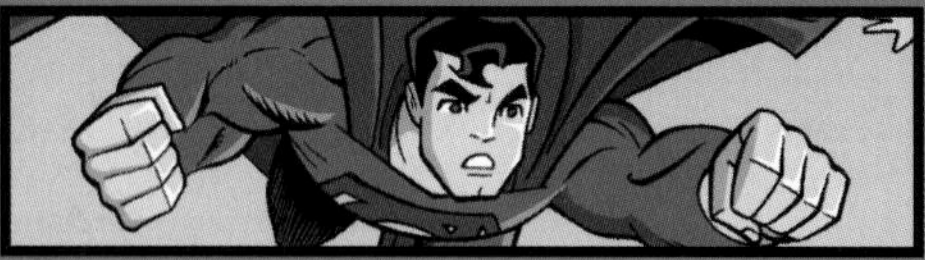

SUPERMAN

Real Name: Clark Kent

Powers: Super-strength, super-speed, flight, super-senses, heat vision, invulnerability, super-breath

Origin: Just before the planet Krypton exploded, baby Kal-EL escaped in a rocket to Earth. On Earth, he was adopted by a kind couple named Jonathan and Martha Kent.

BATMAN

Secret Identity: Bruce Wayne

Abilities: World's greatest detective, acrobat, escape artist

Origin: Orphaned at a young age, young millionaire Bruce Wayne promised to keep all people safe from crime. After training for many years, he put on costume that would scare criminals - the costume of Batman.

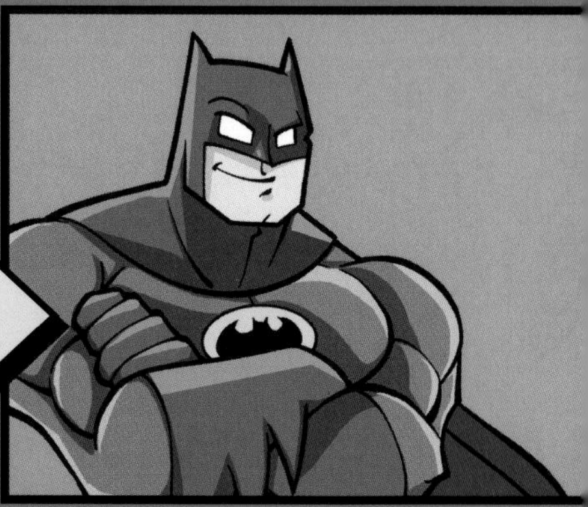

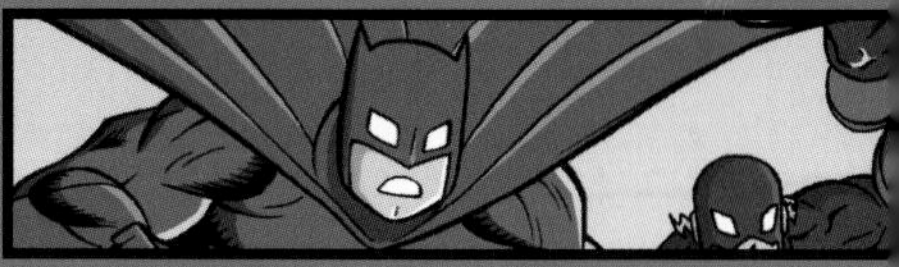

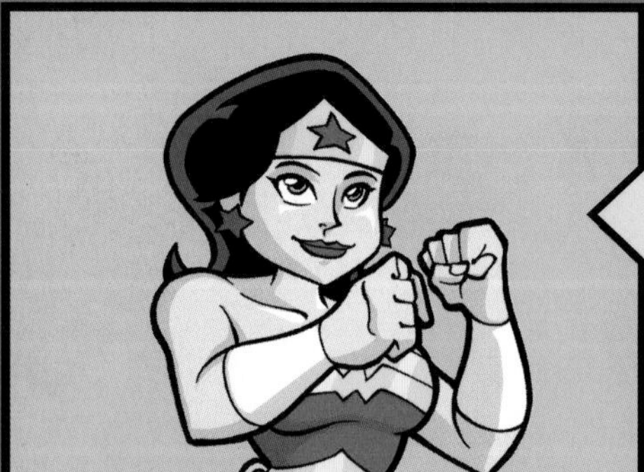

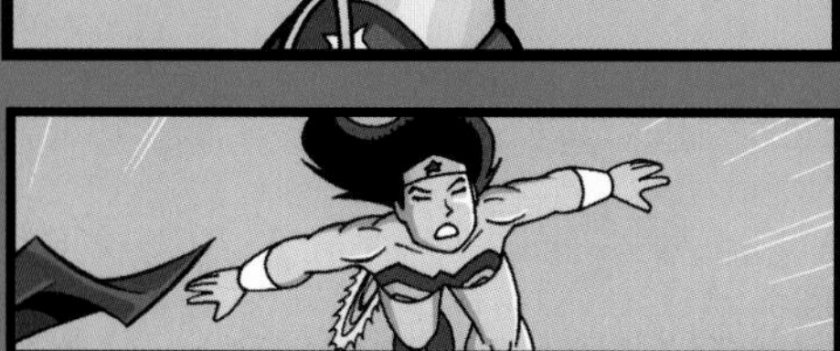

WONDER WOMAN

Secret Identity: Princess Diana

Powers: Super-strong, faster than normal humans, uses her bracelets as shields and magic lasso to make people tell the truth

Origin: Diana is the Princess of Paradise Island, the hidden home of the Amazons. When Diana was a baby, the Greek gods gave her special powers.

GREEN LANTERN

Secret Identity: John Stewart

Powers: Through the strength of willpower, Green Lantern's power ring can create anything he imagines

Origin: Led by the Guardians of the Universe, the Green Lantern Corps is an outer-space police force that keeps the whole universe safe. The Guardians chose John to protect Earth as our planet's Green Lantern.

THE FLASH

Secret Identity: Wally West

Powers: Flash uses his super-speed in many ways: he can run across water or up the side of a building, spin around to make a tornado, or vibrate his body to walk right through a wall

Origin: As a boy, Wally West became the super-fast Kid Flash when lightning hit a rack of chemicals that spilled on him. Today, he helps others as the Flash.

AQUAMAN

Real Name: King Orin or Arthur Curry

Powers: Breathes underwater, communicates with fish, swims at high speed, stronger than normal humans

Origin: Orin's father was a lighthouse keeper and his mother was a mermaid from the undersea land of Atlantis. As Orin grew up, he learned that he could live on land and underwater. He decided to use his powers to keep the seven seas safe as Aquaman.

SHOLLY FISCH WRITER

Bitten by a radioactive typewriter, Sholly Fisch has spent the wee hours writing books, comics, TV scripts, and online material for more than 25 years. His comic book credits include more than 200 stories and features about characters such as Batman, Superman, Bugs Bunny, Daffy Duck, and Ben 10. Currently, he writes stories for Action Comics every month, plus stories for Looney Tunes and Scooby-Doo. By day, Sholly is a mild-mannered developmental psychologist who helps to create educational TV shows, web sites, and other media for kids.

STEWART McKENNY ARTIST

Stewart McKenny is a comic artist living and working in Australia. He has worked on dozens of projects for the world's top comic book publishers, including Dark Horse, Marvel, and DC Comics. His credits include DC Super Friends, Star Wars: Clone Wars Adventures, and Captain America.

PHIL MOY INKER

Phil Moy is a professional comic book and children's book illustrator. He is best known for his work on DC Comics, including Batman: The Brave and the Bold, DC Super Friends, Legion of Super-Heroes in the 31st Century, The Powerpuff Girls, and many more series.

J. BONE COVER ARTIST

J.Bone is a Toronto based illustrator and comic book artist. Besides DC Super Friends, he has worked on comic books such as Spiderman: Tangled Web, Mr. Gum, Gotham Girls, and Madman Adventures. He is also the co-creator of the Alison Dare comic book series.

WOMAN'S *STRENGTH*, BATMAN'S *AGILITY*--

GLOSSARY

acrobats [AK·ruh·bats]–people who perform exciting gymnastic acts that require great skill

boomerang [BOO·muh·rang]–a curved stick that can be thrown through the air so that it returns to the thrower

confusion [kuhn·FYOO·zhuhn]–disorder or chaos

coincidence [koh·IN·si·duhns]–two things that happen at the same time by accident but seem to have some connection

delicate [DEL·uh·kuht]–finely made or sensitive

embarrassing [em·BA·ruh·sing]–causing a feeling of awkwardness or discomfort

emergency [i·MUR·juhn·see]–a sudden and dangerous situation that must be dealt with quickly

imagination [i·maj·uh·NAY·shuhn]–the ability to form pictures in your mind of things that are not present or real

intruders [in·TROO·durs]–people that force their way into a place or situation where they are not wanted or invited

laboratory [LAB·ruh·tor·ee]–a room or building containing special equipment for people to use in scientific experiments

resemble [ri·ZEM·buhl]–to look like someone or something

satellite [SAT·uh·lite]–a spacecraft that is sent into orbit around the Earth, moon, or another heavenly body

unrealistic [uhn·ree·uh·LISS·tik]–not realistic; unlike real life

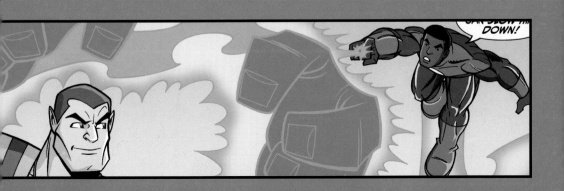

VISUAL QUESTIONS & PROMPTS

1. This panel shows the two men that were at the movies at the beginning of the comic. What clues are there that something is happening to them?

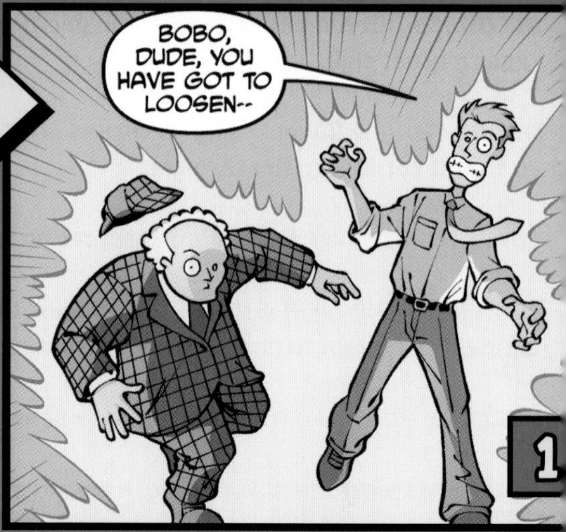
BOBO, DUDE, YOU HAVE GOT TO LOOSEN--
1

2. What can we tell about the Super Friends' powers from this panel?

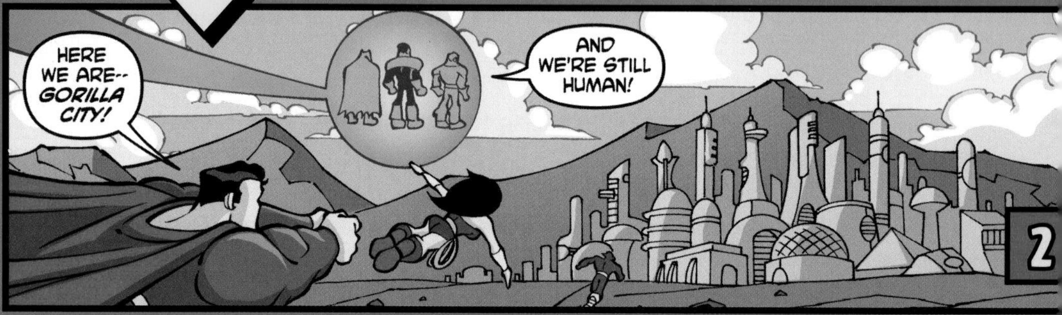
HERE WE ARE-- GORILLA CITY!
AND WE'RE STILL HUMAN!
2

3. Each hero turned into the type of ape that matched their personality. If you were an ape, what type would you be and why?

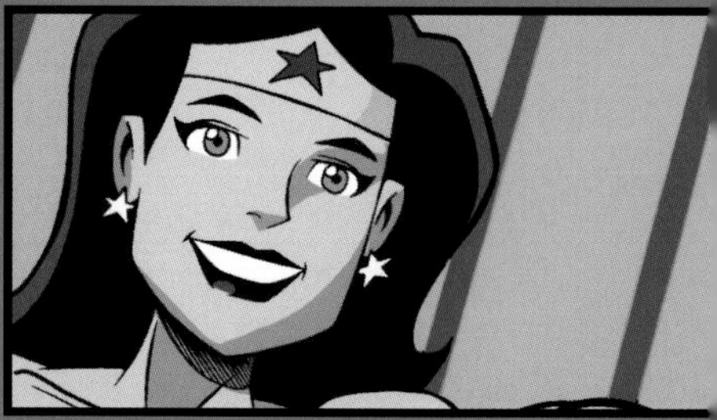

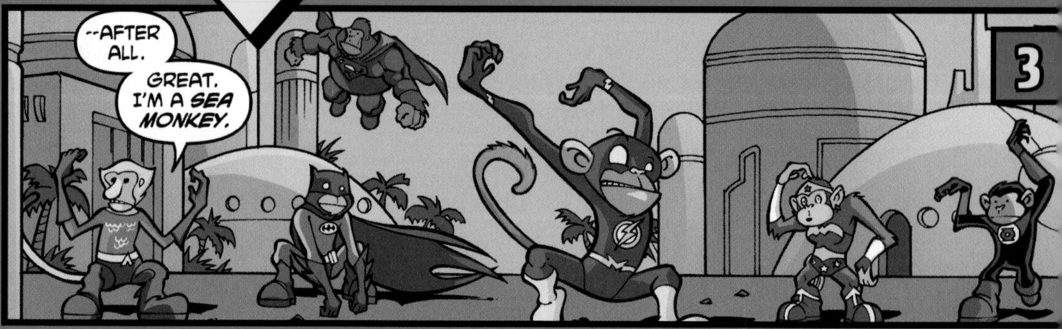
--AFTER ALL.
GREAT. I'M A SEA MONKEY.
3

Lines around a character can sometimes tell you how he or she feels? How does King Solovar feel below?

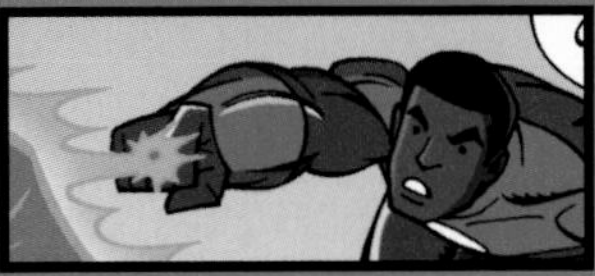

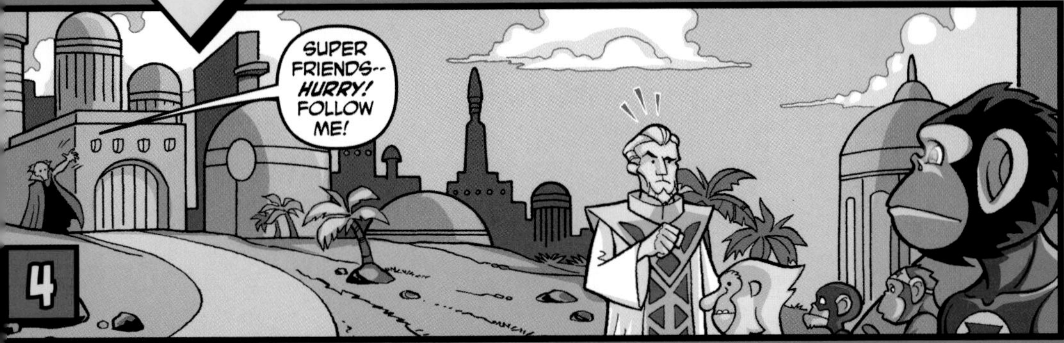
SUPER FRIENDS-- *HURRY!* FOLLOW ME!
4

Think of five sound words that would fit the action of what is happening in this panel.

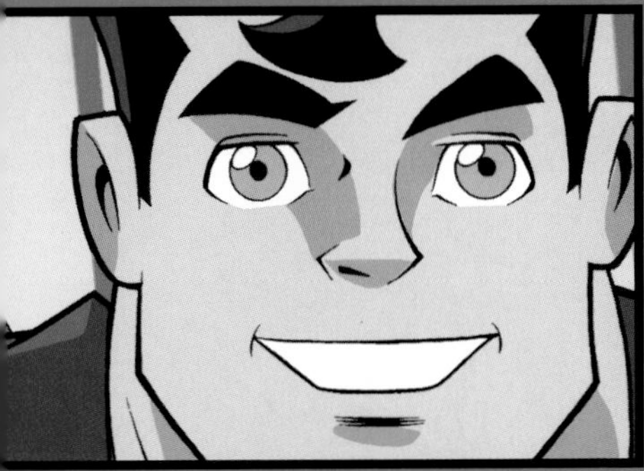

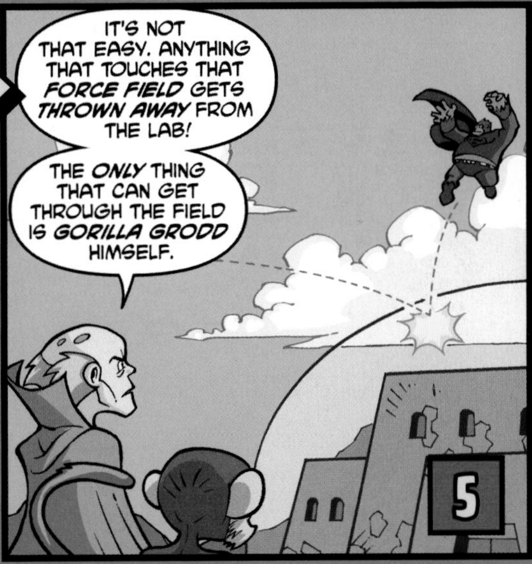
IT'S NOT THAT EASY. ANYTHING THAT TOUCHES THAT *FORCE FIELD* GETS *THROWN AWAY* FROM THE LAB!
THE *ONLY* THING THAT CAN GET THROUGH THE FIELD IS *GORILLA GRODD* HIMSELF.
5

To show that Grodd was thinking about the Anthrotizer, the illustrator placed Grodd's head in the corner of a cloud shaped bubble, with the machine in the middle. What other ways could this idea have been shown?

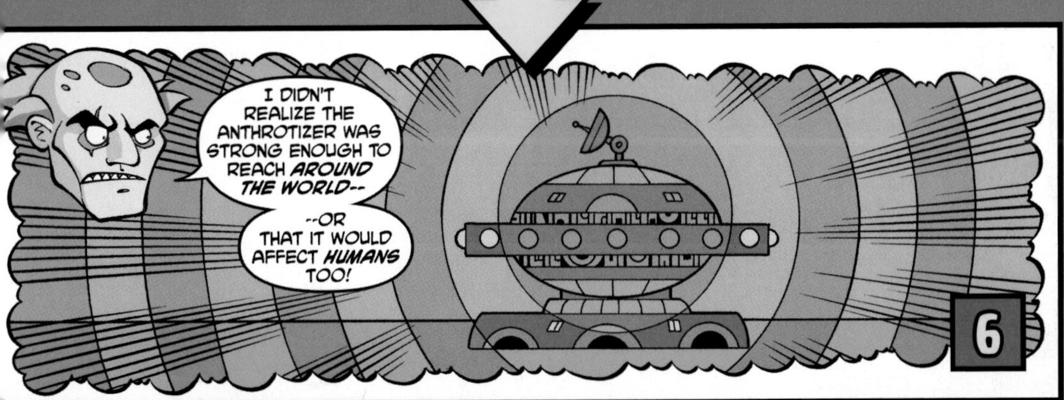
I DIDN'T REALIZE THE ANTHROTIZER WAS STRONG ENOUGH TO REACH *AROUND THE WORLD--*
--OR THAT IT WOULD AFFECT *HUMANS* TOO!
6

READ THEM ALL!

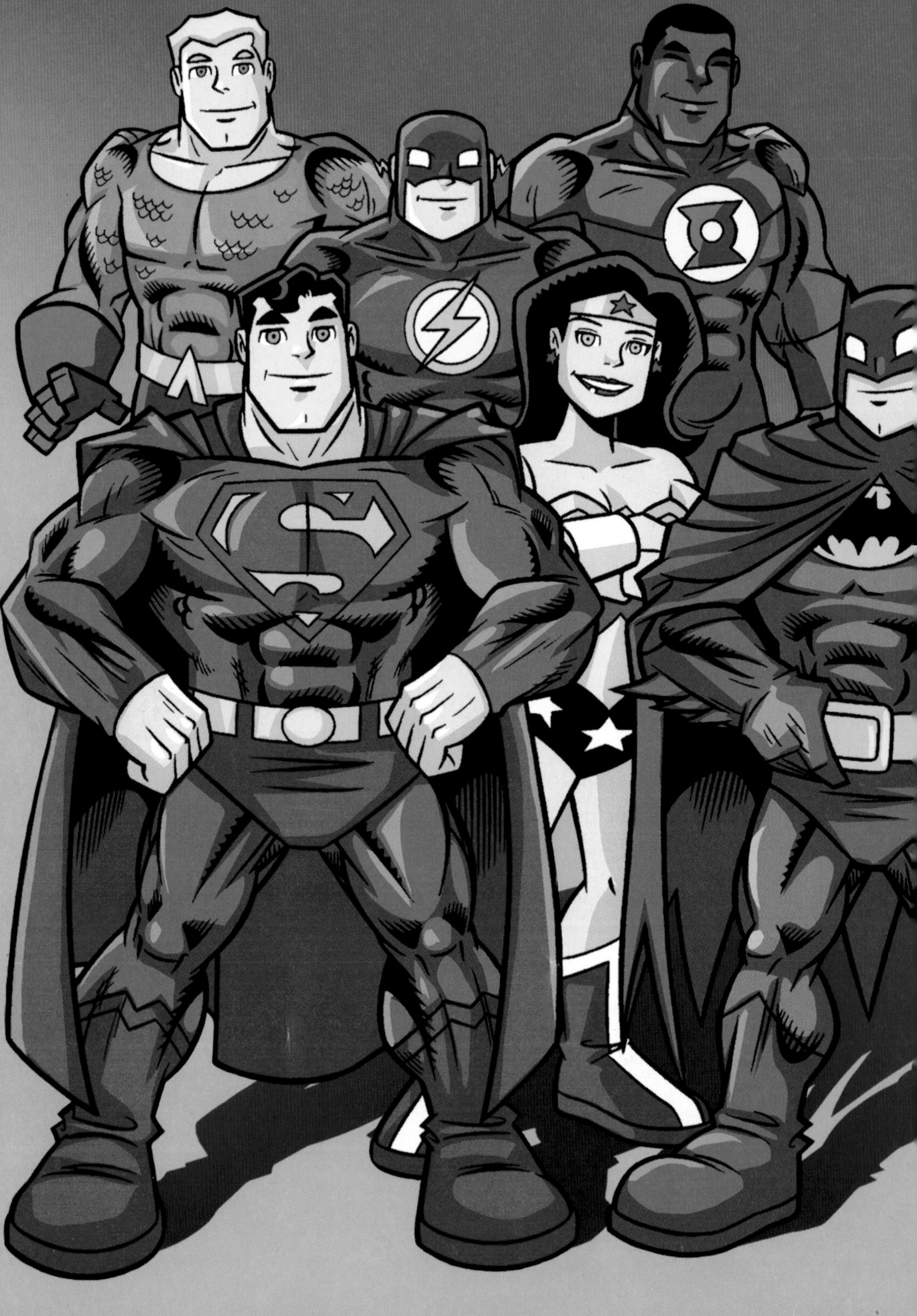

DC SUPER FRIENDS

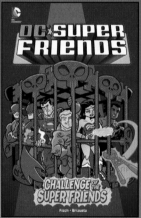

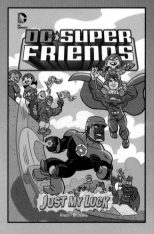